TWINS

written by **VARIAN JOHNSON**
illustrated by **SHANNON WRIGHT**

An Imprint of
■SCHOLASTIC

Library of Congress Control Number: 2019950320

ISBN 978-1-338-23617-0 (hardcover)
ISBN 978-1-338-23613-2 (paperback)

10 9 8 7 6 5 4 3 2 1   20 21 22 23 24

Printed in China   62
First edition, October 2020
Edited by Cassandra Pelham Fulton and Nick Thomas
Book design by Shivana Sookdeo
Creative Director: Phil Falco
Publisher: David Saylor

Sorry, girls, but this one is
for Brad and Andrea

V. J.

For my brothers, Duke and Travis, my
mentor, Kelly, and of course, Brandon

S. W.

TAP! TAP!

Hm...I'm going to be cutting it close for that meeting...

Sorry, Maureen...

Y'all better get out after all.

YESSS!!!

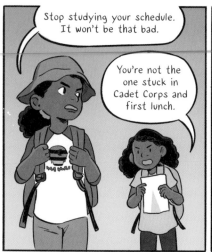

Stop studying your schedule. It won't be that bad.

You're not the one stuck in Cadet Corps and first lunch.

There'll be plenty of other kids who you know in first lunch.

Name three.

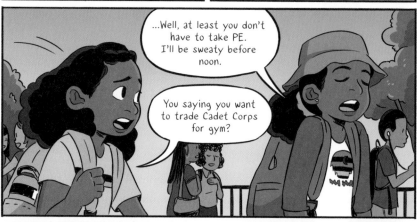

...Well, at least you don't have to take PE. I'll be sweaty before noon.

You saying you want to trade Cadet Corps for gym?

You know me. I look horrible in olive green.

UGH

Why are you so stressed? You're going to ace your classes. You always do.

Yeah, but --

But what? Come on, Maureen. Can't you **try** to pretend you want to be here?

There. Better. Any other problems?

Yeah, you missed a call this morning.

Who? Nikki?

The eighties. They want their hat back.

Hey, Amber! Be honest -- do you like my hat?

Dad had a saying for the two of us.

Throwback! Love it, Maureen!

I'm not --

Never mind. Thanks.

Francine was the talker, and I was the thinker.

You should have asked if she had first lunch.

There's no way I could sit with Amber! And **you** should have asked her.

Well, that's the way it used to be.

WATCH IT!

I can't believe those guys!

Sorry!

We're in middle school now. Only babies dress alike.

Babies. And twins.

Do you know where you're going?!

OUCH !!!

I think advisory is down this hall.

201

202

203

Francine, did you --

RIING!!!

What happened to you?!

Sorry. Guess we got separated.

Quiet down, students. I'm Mrs. Barbosa. Welcome to advisory!

Don't forget to ask about lunch.

Shh!

Savannah?

Here!

Marcus?

Present!

Sydney?

Here!

Francine?

Actually, it's Fran.

Does that make you **Maur**?

Maureen is fine, thank you.

Of course you're supposed to go to class.

Okay, so I report to fifth period, **then** lunch.

You have lunch **between** fourth and fifth period. Young lady, are you trying to be smart?

No, ma'am! I just wasn't sure if I was supposed to go to fifth period and walk to the cafeteria with my class...

We don't hold hands to walk to the cafeteria. You go to lunch, then report to fifth period.

Thanks a lot!

Calm down. It's just lunch. How hard could it be?

I planned it all out during science class. I figured my best chance of eating lunch with someone I knew was to catch them before they entered the cafeteria.

I knew some of the kids...

TOO LOUD

TOO MEAN

TOO POPULAR

TOO DIVA

WON'T REMEMBER ME

THROWS FOOD

In the end, no one seemed like a good fit.

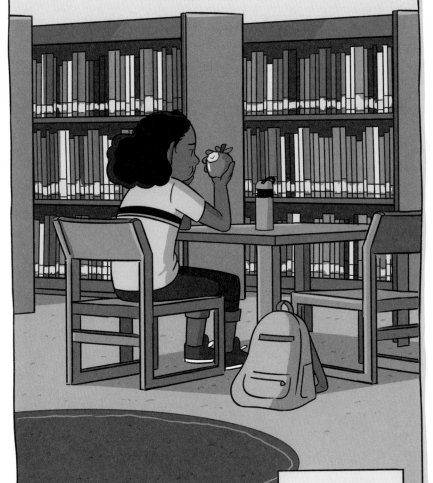

NO-MAN'S-LAND

I knew I could go to the library during lunch.

I am Master Sergeant Lucinda Fields.

Your instructor for the Youth Cadet Corps program.

At least I knew some kids in Cadet Corps.

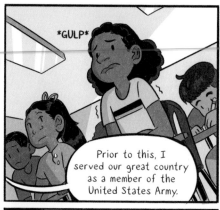

GULP

Prior to this, I served our great country as a member of the United States Army.

I did many tours abroad. Afghanistan. Korea.

CADET! GIVE ME TEN!

AHHHHH!!!!!

Dollars?

Address me as Master Sergeant or ma'am. And I'm talking about push-ups, Cadet.

Now get to it before I add ten more.

26

Those of you new to YCC will begin as cadets.

There will be opportunities to earn rank throughout the year.

One...two...three...

Your class leader is Private First Class Bryce Jackson.

Private, come up and brief the cadets on our procedures.

Eight...nine...ten!!!

Good job, Garcia. Go ahead and take a seat.

??

Good job! Tomorrow we'll try **real** marching!

PANT

HUFF

SQUAD, DISMISSED!

That was fun!

You **like** marching?

Better than running around the gym all year.

Hey, sorry we didn't have room for you at lunch. Where'd you end up sitting?

I, um, found a quiet spot.

Oh, good.

GULP!

I was worried that you ended up by yourself in the library or something.

SPIT!

Talk about depressing!

My legs were still sore when I got home.

...But by far, my favorite class was chorus.

I fall between soprano and alto. Ms. Ryan put me with altos for now.

And I think I'm going to run for student council.

Maybe even pres --

I want to hear all about it, honey. But let's give Maureen a chance to talk about her day, okay?

My day was fine.

I liked coding class.

What about Cadet Corps? They promote you to captain yet?

It was... sweaty.

But speaking of that...

In math, Julia told me she was switching PE for Cadet Corps, so I thought, maybe I could take **her** spot in PE.

It's the same time Francine has PE. We'd be in another class together!

I think you should give Cadet Corps a shot. You might really like it.

RING! RING! RING!

~Ugh

CLICK

Too bright!

You can't hide in bed forever.

Should I wear the red or blue?

Maureen?

Francine was right about some things. Science class was a lot better on Tuesday.

We form a hypothesis!

Correct!

And language arts was better on Wednesday.

Watch out, Maya Angelou! Here comes Maureen Carter!

I even found ways to see my friends between classes.

I'm going to the mall with Nikki and Tasha after school. Wanna come?

I'll check with Francine.

Okay! Don't leave me hanging!

But Francine wasn't right about everything.

No. Why?

Then it's going great!

Maureen...

It's just... hard.

Hang in there. It'll get better.

That's what everyone keeps saying.

Anything I can do to cheer you up?

Actually, yeah. Can I borrow your phone?

My mom tried to give me a big speech, too! We're not babies!

NOD NOD NOD

I know! We can walk around the mall by ourselves!

You saved Curtis's number in your phone, right?

NOD

Hey. No Fran?

TAP TAP

I don't know where **Francine** is. She had other plans.

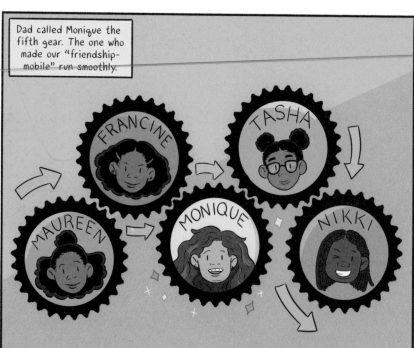

Dad called Monique the fifth gear. The one who made our "friendship-mobile" run smoothly.

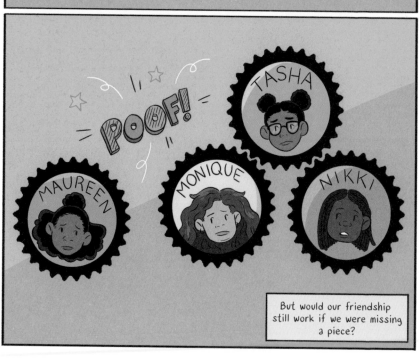

But would our friendship still work if we were missing a piece?

Y'all go ahead. We'll wait here.

You can stop with all the pretend smiling, Maureen.

I'm not --

You don't wanna be here any more than I do. At least I can fake it better than you.

So why come if you don't want to be here?

Now that Angela's in college, the house is too quiet.

And if I have to pick between being bored at home or walking around the mall...

Well, I pick the mall.

I guess...

51

Well, it was **kind of** fun.

If I have to pick between being bored at home or walking around the mall, I pick the mall.

I guess.

Or maybe you just need more hobbies.

She hates us.

You're exaggerating.

Fine. She hates **me.**

Come on! Can't you lie to make me feel better?

HA HA HA HA HA

Our creed says we're not supposed to lie.

Somebody's been reading their manual.

She's just giving you a hard time, Garcia. She doesn't hate anyone.

Well, except Nazis.

Was she joking about drill five days a week?

Afraid not. It's important. Drill is twenty percent of our grade.

Don't worry, though!

Master Sergeant Fields has never failed anyone for not being able to march!

Cadet Carter. Do you have a second?

She hasn't failed anyone for being bad at drill, but it could drop you from an A to a B.

Or worse.

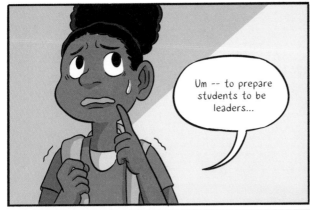

Um -- to prepare students to be leaders...

SIGH

...With a commitment to discipline, self-confidence, integrity, and...betterment of self and community.

I see why you graduated number one in elementary school.

clap *clap*

I did?

I could assign you twenty extra-credit essays and I bet you'd ace each one.

But that wouldn't help you fulfill our mission, right?

I thought they didn't track our rank...

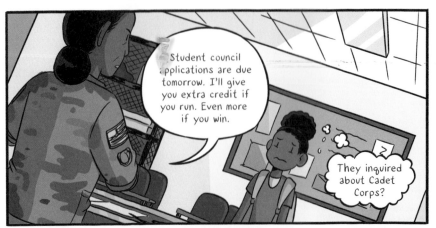

Student council applications are due tomorrow. I'll give you extra credit if you run. Even more if you win.

They inquired about Cadet Corps?

What do you say?

Yes, ma'am. Thank you, Master Sergeant.

Um, Master Sergeant... what do you mean my parents **inquired** about YCC?

Careful with the door, Maureen. Don't want to hurt the car's feelings.

Any idea where your sister is?

Oh, I remember! She's got a thing this afternoon.

Guess it's just us.

How long am I going to drive before you tell me what's wrong?

Hormones.

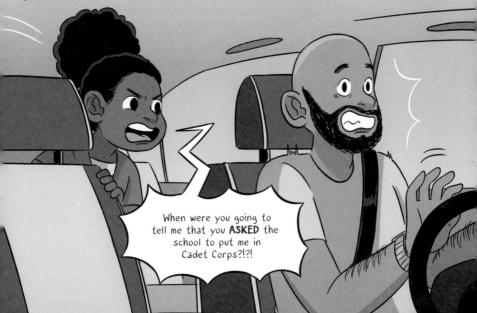
When were you going to tell me that you **ASKED** the school to put me in Cadet Corps?!?!

CHAPTER 3

Sorry. Anyway, it **wasn't** a computer fluke that gave us different schedules.

Mom and Dad **asked** the school to do it!

And they stuck me in Cadet Corps because they don't think I have high self-confidence!

Can you believe it?!

But we can fix our schedules. You should probably switch to my Spanish and social studies classes.

I already have a partner for our class project, but I'm sure Penelope will understand if --

Maureen...

I don't want to change my schedule.

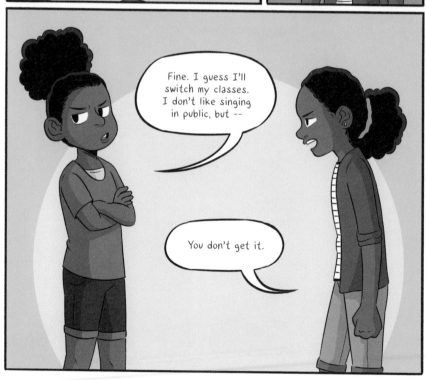

Fine. I guess I'll switch my classes. I don't like singing in public, but --

You don't get it.

Sleep on it. You'll feel better in the morning.

And tomorrow, maybe I can run some ideas for my campaign by you. I could use your help.

If you really wanted my help, you would ask me to be on your planning committee instead of meeting after school without me.

That's not why --

My bad. I **totally** want your help. You're the smartest person I know. With your help, I'm a shoo-in.

I, um...I was thinking about running for student council. But I guess you don't want me to...

No! It's not that I don't want to do anything with you. Just not **everything.**

What position? Treasurer, since you're so good at math? That'll boost your self-confidence for sure.

We can help each other with our platforms!

You'll have to give a speech in front of the school.

I know you hate public speaking.

Like I said, I was sick the morning of that speech.

Sure, sure...but still, you haven't tried to talk to a big group since then.

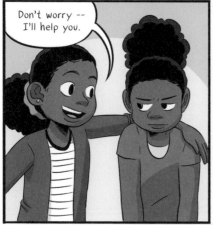

Don't worry -- I'll help you.

That's what big sisters are for, right?

Wow!

Looking sharp, Cadet!

Thanks.

So, about yesterday...

Francine and I talked. We're keeping separate schedules.

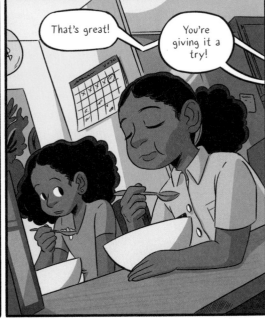

That's great!

You're giving it a try!

Thanks again for understanding. You're the best sister a girl could ask for.

I'm late for a meeting!

Be sure to put in your application for treasurer!

Ugh.

Cadet Carter!

Hey, Bryce. I mean -- Private First Class Jackson.

Oops!

And you can just address me as Private Jackson, Cadet.

The uniform looks good on you!

Makes you look taller! Sharper!

See you in class!

6th GRADE

O'CONNOR MIDDLE SCHOOL

NAME: _Maureen Carter_

ADVISORY TEACHER: _Mrs. Barbosa_

POSITION RUNNING FOR:

⬭ PRESIDENT ⬭

VICE PRESIDENT

SECRETARY

TREASURER

HISTORIAN

CHAPTER 4

I planned to tell Francine about class elections first thing Saturday morning.

Then she ditched me to hang with her chorus friends.

10:03 AM

10:27 AM

10:56 AM

Eventually I called around to see what everyone was up to. Monique wasn't home, so I called Nikki.

I'd caught them as they were heading to the mall.

It was nice being with people who actually **wanted** to spend time with me.

Where are all the boys?!?!

Well, you did ask for boys...

Fine. Let's go shopping.

Come on, Nikki.

I mean, it's not like you actually want to **talk** to them.

This is pretty! But I need a different size.

Must be nice to have a big allowance.

I'm getting the sudden urge to spend my money elsewhere.

Girls, I suggest you do the same.

TURN

Wait, I...

Mom...

I was glad Nikki's mom had decided to "hang out" nearby.

Just in case we needed her.

Just in case something went wrong.

Mercy DAN

If you think you can treat my girls any old way!

You have no right!!

I need to speak to a manager!!!

I told Mom what happened once I got home.

S%#&%!!!

She was a bit more colorful than Nikki's mom.

It was safe to say that we weren't ever shopping at Mercy Danger again.

I planned to tell Francine about it that night. About that... and the election.

Maureen? You awake?

But I was already asleep by the time she got home.

On Sunday, I promised God that I was going to tell Francine soon. Like after church.

Though, technically, I didn't say **immediately** after church.

After the service, we went to my favorite restaurant, the Wonderful World of Waffles.

And who wants to talk about election stuff while eating waffles?

At home, Curtis gave us a new game.

Francine even let me have first dibs.

I still want to talk to you about my platform. Have you thought about yours?

Um, I've got a few ideas.

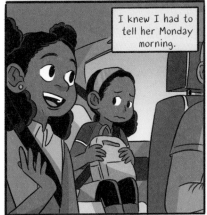

I knew I had to tell her Monday morning.

But maybe when she was by herself. I didn't want to make a scene.

There's something you should --

That left advisory.

Teachers, please send all sixth-grade students running for student council to the library.

Time to meet the competition.

HEHEHE

GULP

Hello! I'm Mr. Wilson, your adviser for sixth-grade student council.

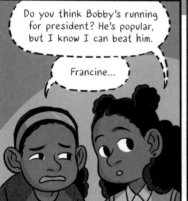

Do you think Bobby's running for president? He's popular, but I know I can beat him.

Francine...

Let's make sure everyone's here.

Hmmm.

Here goes!

This is interesting. We only have two students running for president.

What's your platform? Who's on your campaign committee?

I haven't really thought that far...

Well, count me in! I'm too chicken to run, but I have plenty of ideas!

You, chicken?

I also get extra credit in social studies if I help with a campaign.

Want to talk about it at lunch? We'll save you a seat at our table!

Okay?

Francine didn't speak to me that afternoon, either.

She'd have to talk to me eventually.

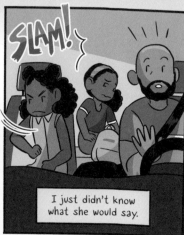

SLAM!

I just didn't know what she would say.

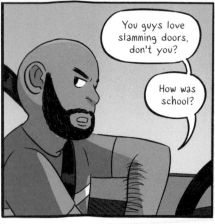

You guys love slamming doors, don't you?

How was school?

So your Mom and I talked...

And since you guys have been so mature, especially about the schedule thing...

We decided to give you cell phones! Isn't that great?!

So, what do you think?

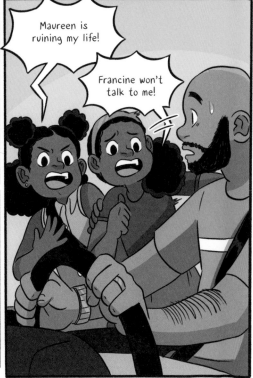

Maureen is ruining my life!

Francine won't talk to me!

105

But why president, Maureen? Fran has been talking about running since school began.

It feels disingenuous not to be honest about your intentions.

Oh, you mean disingenuous like how y'all put us in separate classes.

And then LIED about it?

Well, we **did** get you a cell phone...

So then are you only running because you're mad?

No. I have good ideas. I'm a leader -- whether you think so or not. I have a campaign committee and everything.

Quit if you don't want to run against me. Or what -- are you scared of a little competition?

Me? Scared?

Well, it **could** be good...

For both of them...

Okay. Clearly you both have the right to run. I don't like it...but we won't force either of you to drop out.

As long as you keep it civil.

No arguing at school. No smear campaigns.

If we find out you two are acting like anything other than sisters, you'll lose a lot more than those cell phones.

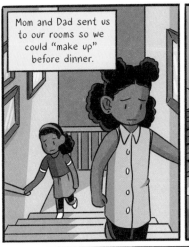

Mom and Dad sent us to our rooms so we could "make up" before dinner.

Why didn't you tell me?

FLOP!

I tried. But I didn't know how.

Plus, I was mad when you said I had no self-confidence. Or low. Whatever.

SIGH

I know I was being mean when you said you wanted to change schedules.

I just...I'm tired of competing against you.

What are you talking about? We don't compete against each other. I mean, other than in video games.

One of us would stay in our room.

The other would take Curtis's room.

Dad made us flip for it.

FLIP!!!

SNATCH!

SLAP!

Guess who lost.

I'll move the rest of my clothes tomorrow.

You don't have to move **everything**.

What about these? You can keep them for now. I'll take them next week.

Stop acting like we're getting divorced. You can come back to the room anytime you want.

You mean, except when you're on the phone. Or when you want your space.

You're not going to guilt me into feeling sorry for you.

Hm. I thought leaders were supposed to be compassionate.

It's just a stupid room! Why are you making such a big deal about everything?!

Because everything **IS** a big deal! We've never even slept ap--

I didn't have to finish. She knew what I was going to say.

Francine and I had never slept apart before.

We'd always shared a room. At camp. At our grandparents' house...

Even on that road trip where we shared a bed at every stop and Francine kept kneeing me in my back.

I could have slept with Grandma, but didn't.

The way Dad tells it...

ERRR!!!

The game was rigged.

It took a while, but Dad eventually figured out how to win.

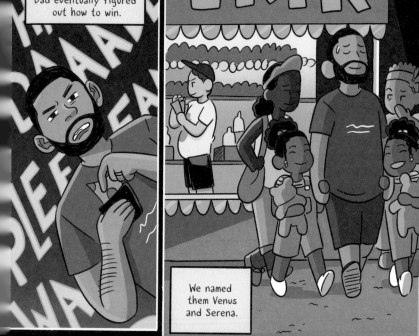

We named them Venus and Serena.

Since then, they'd traveled everywhere with us.

No, I think they'll be lonely without each other.

Thinking about taking Serena?

Wait! One last thing...

Whatever you do, **don't** open Curtis's top drawer.

SLAM!!

SWOOP!

CLICK!

Do, re, mi, fa --

YAAAWN~

Gotta run. Bye!

Then Mr. Harvey marched up to him...

And was like, "Why aren't you playing what's on the sheet music?"

"I don't know how to read sheet music!!"

And the newbie was like, "I'm a drummer..."

HA HA HA HA HA HA

Maureen!

LET'S TALK STRATEGY!

I heard you were running for class president. Good luck!

We're working on campaign ideas. Any suggestions?

No, but I'll let you know if I think of something.

While I'm here...study up on chapter one of your handbook. Master Sergeant always puts military history on the first exam.

Just something I wish I'd known as a first-year cadet.

That was nice of him to say.

He wasn't **that** nice. It's just his job.

Right, Maureen?

Maureen...?

Bryce! Got a second?

What else do you wish you knew when you were a sixth grader?

Not just cadet stuff. Everything.

Well, lunch on the first day was pretty confusing.

EXACTLY!

And I didn't know we were supposed to dress up for the October dance.

There's a dance in October?

I can probably make a list --

Is the seventh-grade president nice? Like you? Or are you only nice because you have to be?

I'm not nice because I have to be. I like being nice to you...

To all of you, I mean...

cough

But yeah, Rhonda, the seventh-grade president, is really nice, too.

I think it would be cool if there was a way to buddy up sixth graders with seventh graders.

Do you think she'd be open to talking about it?

One way to find out.

Come on. I'll introduce you.

If it helps, I think it's a great idea.

And just like that, I had a platform.

Once we had the nuts and bolts of the platform, it was time to make posters.

Mom, this is Amber and Richard.

Hello! Nice to meet you kids!

I didn't realize you invited **new** friends over! That's great! But what about Nikki and Tasha?

They're staying out of the race. They don't want to choose sides. Not like Monique.

Be nice...

Do you mind working in your bedroom? Rachel is stopping by and I don't want to bore you with our conversation.

Ooh! That means y'all are talking about something juicy!

Any idea how Fran's campaign is going?

Not sure. We haven't really discussed it.

It must be weird running against your sister.

Twin sister.

Yeah. Double weird.

What if you and Fran come up with the same platform?!

I don't think that'll happen.

But don't you guys share the same thoughts? You know, like twin psychic powers?

HAHAHAHA
HAHA HAHA

It's not funny! I swear, I saw it on TV!

All joking aside, Richard does bring up a good point.

We need a way to make you stand out from Fran. Kids have to know they're voting for you, not her.

NOD NOD

What about a photo?

Yeah, but not just any photo.

Nothing gets votes like a girl in uniform!

We should use some of these photos as well.

What about this one?

BUZZZ!!!

BUZZ! BUZZ!

Monique 😺☆

Hey! Sorry for this morning

Got time to talk now?

Do you need to get that?

It's not important.

The essay contest?

That photo makes me want to throw up. Literally.

You're being dramatic. We should take a vote.

Everyone who thinks we should use it, say aye.

SIGH

But --

AYE!!!

Done! The ayes have it!

SIGH

We didn't think it would be a problem to post photos of me in my uniform, but Amber made me check, just in case.

These look good, Cadet. I like how you squared your shoulders.

Also, exemplary job on your exam yesterday. It's evident that you studied.

Thank you, ma'am.

You'd be the perfect cadet -- if I could teach you how to march.

FIELDS

Let me guess -- you've never received anything less than an A in a class.

No, ma'am. Not on a report card.

A B isn't the worst grade in the world, Cadet.

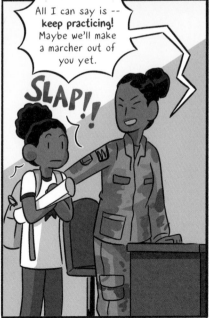

All I can say is -- **keep practicing!** Maybe we'll make a marcher out of you yet.

SLAP!!

I tried extra hard at drill practice that afternoon.

At least I didn't fall.

This time.

Hang in there. You really are getting better.

What's the point of running for president if I won't get enough extra credit for an A?

Is that the only reason you're running?

Not the only reason...

But aren't you serving on my campaign committee just for the extra credit?

Okay, yeah. I was at first. But now I'm doing it because I'm your friend.

Don't get me wrong, though -- the extra credit helps. Me and social studies don't mix.

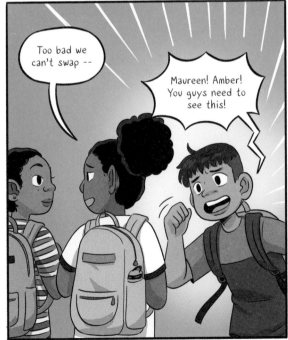

Too bad we can't swap --

Maureen! Amber! You guys need to see this!

Lucky for me, I made it to the bathroom in time.

BLUURG!!

But I didn't make it to a stall.

sniff

Francine found me a few minutes later.

sniff
sniff

She tried to get me to go back onstage, but I couldn't.

So we came up with another plan.

I mean, we were identical twins. Who would know?

Francine was amazing. She sounded better than I ever had delivering the speech.

She didn't even need to look at my paper. She'd heard it so many times, she had memorized it.

I never told any of my friends what happened. I didn't tell a teacher, either. Or our parents. I was too embarrassed.

We promised to keep it a secret.

Francine promised.

As soon as I saw Francine, I knew.

And she knew I knew.

Richard was right.

Sometimes we **could** read each other's minds.

I thought about confronting her then, but decided not to.

Curtis was coming over for dinner tonight.

I wanted them all to hear it at the same time.

CHAPTER 7

Maureen, Francine -- you two are pretty quiet. Don't like my cooking?

Like that's ever stopped them.

So... how's the election coming along?

Do you want to tell them, or should I?

I don't know what --

Don't. Just don't.

You promised -- no dirty politics.

No -- you were just telling all my secrets to your gym class!

It was an accident! I didn't mean to hurt you!

Well, you did!

YANK!

Look, if you hadn't run in the first place --

CLAP!

CLAP!

Enough!!!

We're going to try this again. From the beginning.

Without all the yelling.

Mom and Dad were surprised to hear about how Francine and I swapped places for my speech. I think Dad even found it funny.

Then I told them about the poster.

How it looked. How everyone stared and laughed.

How I felt.

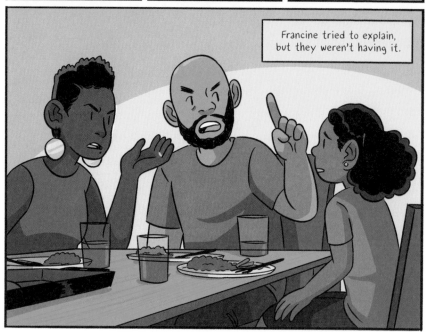

Francine tried to explain, but they weren't having it.

Francine, we are very, very disappointed in you. She is your sister.

You had no right to share her secret.

But --

Maureen, do you want Francine to report this to the school?

It may help them determine who actually vandalized your poster.

I just want to forget it ever happened.

And I don't want her to get into that much trouble.

That's very kind of you. But, Francine, that doesn't mean you're off the hook.

You're grounded indefinitely.

And, of course, you'll be dropping out of the election.

DAD!

Your mother and I aren't going to let you two tear each other apart over a silly election.

It's not silly.

You broke the rules, Francine. That has consequences.

With Francine out, I was guaranteed a win. No more posters or platforms. Maybe I wouldn't even have to give a speech.

That felt like cheating.

And most of the students wouldn't know I won. A vote for me would be like a vote for her. It would be like voting for the same person.

Francine didn't want me to live in her shadow anymore.

I didn't want to live there, either.

I don't want Francine to drop out.

That's nice of you, but you don't owe your sister anything in this matter.

And, quite frankly, it isn't your decision.

But if she doesn't run I'll never know...

I'll never know if I was good enough to win on my own.

Are you sure?

Yeah, I am.

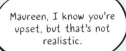

Maureen, I know you're upset, but that's not realistic.

Why not? Dad's always joking about moving us all out as soon as possible.

Um...your mother and I need to discuss --

scratch
scratch

I'll do it.

I caused all this mess. It's the least I can do.

That is, if it's okay with Curtis.

Um...sure? I guess that wouldn't be a problem. I mean --

ENOUGH!

I am not kicking one of my girls out of the house over this election!

But --

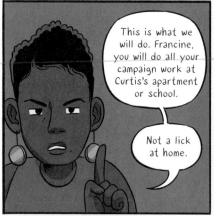

This is what we will do. Francine, you will do all your campaign work at Curtis's apartment or school.

Not a lick at home.

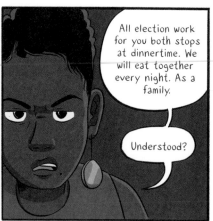

All election work for you both stops at dinnertime. We will eat together every night. As a family.

Understood?

NOD NOD

Yes, ma'am.

NOD NOD

Yes, Mom.

Curtis, does this work for you? Do you want to think it over?

It'll be okay, Diane. It really isn't any trouble.

scratch *scratch*

But, um, when exactly is this election again?

After dinner, Francine went to pack up her election materials.

That was really nice, what you did for Francine.

It wasn't just for her.

Is school getting any better? Want to talk about it?

Things are good. I have a lot of friends.

Well, two -- Amber and Richard. And I guess Bryce is my friend, too.

What about Nikki, Tasha, and Monique?

SPLASH!

Duh! Of course they are!

Or, hey -- it's cool if you have a thing for Amber! Just don't go kissing anybody yet.

Plenty of time for that!

CURTIS! I don't want to kiss ANYONE!

I need to meet these friends of yours. Give them my stamp of approval.

You had your chance. They were here the other day when you dropped Francine off.

They were here? Where?

Don't worry, they weren't in your room.

SIGH

And even if they were, they would have never peeked in your top right dresser drawer.

But for real -- why didn't you tell me that you and Francine were hanging out? Y'all go to the mall?

It must have slipped my mind. I'll take you this weekend if you want to go. Just call and --

cough

Here's everything.

I guess I'll see you tomorrow?

Guys, I know things are difficult right now.

Just don't forget, y'all are sisters.

Bye, Dad! Bye, Diane! Thanks for dinner!

CLICK!

Need help with the dishes?

No, thanks. Almost done.

Are you sure? I can --

I'm good.

I know you don't believe me, but I promise, I'll find out who drew that picture on your poster.

I don't even care anymore.

And I'm still game for moving into Curtis's room.

Don't go doing me any favors. I'm fine where I am.

BUUZZZ!!!

Maureen! Please! I just --

BUUZZ!!!

Hey, Amber. Yeah, now's a good time to talk.

I wasn't doing anything important.

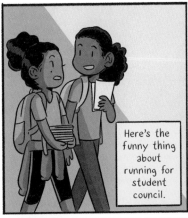

CHAPTER 8

Here's the funny thing about running for student council.

Most kids didn't really care about the election. Some would at least pretend to be interested.

Others, not so much.

But some kids did care.

And those kids seemed to really like my idea for a school buddy system.

Thank you!

Of course, my idea wasn't the only good one.

Francine's platform was all about more interaction between clubs at school.

Like asking the chorus to sing while the orchestra accompanied them.

WANT YOUR CLUB TO BE SEEN? THEN VOTE 4 FRAN!

Or having the drama club perform skits at halftime during the basketball games.

She even suggested "Showcase Days" where clubs could perform during lunch.

Don't worry. Who wants to perform in front of a big group, anyway?

Oh, I don't know. Maybe the chorus. Or the band. Or the drama club...

Can't you do that program after you win? Your sister wouldn't mind, right?

Not sure, I'll have to ask her.

Once I start talking to her.

Don't take this the wrong way, but it would be kind of cool to do drill performances with a live band.

GRRR

What are traits of a good leader?

Communication?

Unlike me and Richard, Amber was acing Cadet Corps inside and outside the classroom.

Good job, Cadet. Any other --

Garcia, are you drawing again?!

You know the drill.

Though marching was the least of Richard's problems.

We'd be friends like before.

I mean, it's not like you and Fran will stop being sisters once you win the election.

She'd probably even be happy for you if you won. And you'd be happy for her. Right?

Yeah, I'd be happy.

Wouldn't I?

Bye, Curtis! See you tomorrow.

Curtis isn't coming in?

He's got plans with friends tonight.

Good. He can eat someone else out of house and home.

Go on and wash your hands. Food's about ready.

But I ate at --

Then eat again.

HeHeHe

Maureen, don't test your luck.

But how...?

Mom-sense. Works every time.

190

Francine started to talk...

And talk...

And talk.

I couldn't lie. For a second I even thought about voting for her.

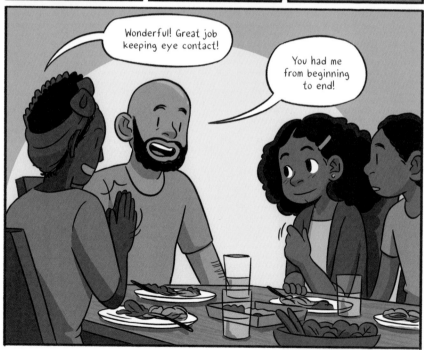

Wonderful! Great job keeping eye contact!

You had me from beginning to end!

Your turn, Maureen.

Picture us as your audience!

I wish he hadn't said that.

My platform is to form a...buddy system...

Where a sixth grader is paired with an, um, older kid. You know, probably a seventh grader.

Or maybe an eighth grader? I, uh, haven't worked out those details yet...

Anyway, it's to help prepare us sixth graders for middle school...

That's a wonderful idea!

Awesome! You've got me hooked!

Yeah. Good platform, Maureen.

Can't you at least say it like you mean it?!

I do mean it! It's a good idea!

Everyone knows you always come up with the best ideas.

CHAPTER 9

For the next couple days, Francine and I did our best to steer clear of each other.

Dad said that things would return to normal once the election was over.

But that seemed impossible.

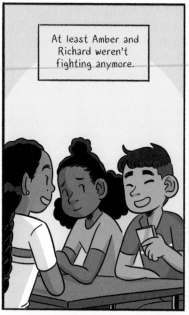

At least Amber and Richard weren't fighting anymore.

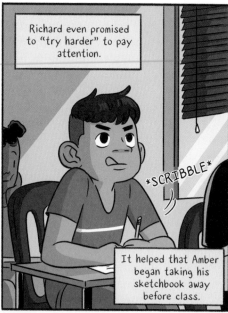

Richard even promised to "try harder" to pay attention.

SCRIBBLE

It helped that Amber began taking his sketchbook away before class.

And thanks to Amber's help, I was getting better at drill...

Good form, Cadet. You've been practicing.

OOF!

But maybe not good enough.

Hey, Maureen!

Are you looking for Francine? If so, she's --

Can we please stop. Okay?

Nikki and Tasha are coming over on Friday night.

I know things have been weird between us, but I want you to come, too.

Will **Fran** be there?

Funny.

Fran asked the same question about you.

Come on. I want it to be like before.

But everybody's different now! And not just Francine. Nikki and Tasha are always with their band friends.

And you --

Wait, what did I do?

You chose Francine's committee. You picked her over me.

Maureen...

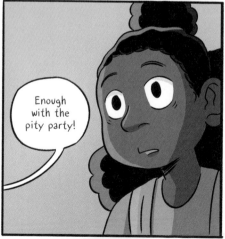

Enough with the pity party!

It's not like you don't have other friends, too!

Yeah, but --

I didn't know you planned to run when I joined Fran's committee. None of us knew, remember?

I almost quit, but I didn't want to abandon Fran. Nikki and Tasha had already quit in order to be fair to you.

I didn't know they were on her committee in the first place.

Of course they were. We all were.

I wasn't! She never asked me!

You're sisters. She didn't think she **needed** to ask.

H O N K!

I shouldn't say this... but ask Fran what she does when she's not working on election stuff.

Here's a hint-- she's usually at school, but not hanging with friends.

I don't understand. You mean she's practicing with chorus?

Maureen!

Chorus is not an after-school activity.

HONK! HONK!

MONIQUE!

Coming, Mama!

TAP TAP

9
10
11
12

Hey! Where were you?

I tried to call, but --

Master Sergeant Fields told me I graduated at the top of my fifth-grade class.

She did? Well, those are just unofficial rankings.

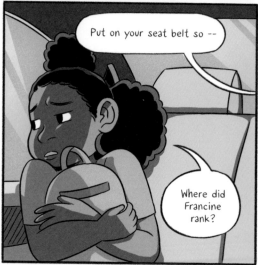

Put on your seat belt so --

Where did Francine rank?

It wasn't even a real graduation. And it's not really any of your --

Was she second? Third?

Why are you asking this?

Because I know Francine's getting tutored after school!

≡SIGH≡

When did you find out?

Just now.

Fran was tenth.

Really? That's not bad!

Of course it's not! Your mother and I are very proud of Fran and the work she's doing.

Me too! And like you said, it's unofficial! It doesn't mean anything!

It means a lot when it's your twin who was ranked number one.

Put on your seat belt.

Let's go home.

O'CONNOR MIDDLE SCHOOL

This had been going on for a lot longer than sixth grade.

Dad told me you found out.

Yeah. This afternoon.

I thought I recognized that ringtone.

PLOP!

Look, don't go making a big deal out of --

I'M SORRY FOR RUNNING FOR PRESIDENT!

Huh?!

I ran for the wrong reasons. I was mad.

And hurt.

PLOP!

It felt like you were throwing me away...

I should have told you about the class schedules.

But I was afraid that if I said anything, you'd convince me to change my mind.

Maureen, remember how Dad used to say that you were the thinker and I was the talker?

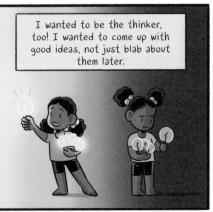

I wanted to be the thinker, too! I wanted to come up with good ideas, not just blab about them later.

But the worst was when everyone thought it was you who gave that speech for Earth Day.

There I was, finally good at something.

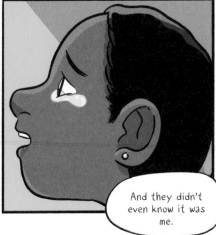

And they didn't even know it was me.

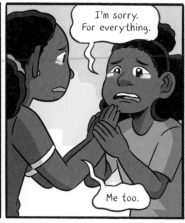

I'm sorry. For everything.

Me too.

I'll drop out if you want me to.

Are you still running only to get back at me?

Not anymore. I like my platform!

It's a good idea!

Yours is, too!

Francine and I decided not to go to Monique's house on Friday night.

Instead, we worked on our speeches.

We read them to our parents and Curtis on Saturday.

And on Sunday, we read them to our campaign committees.

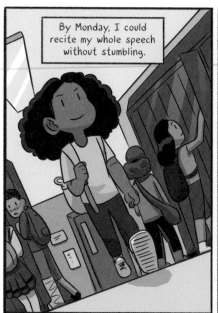

By Monday, I could recite my whole speech without stumbling.

KNOCK! KNOCK!

It was almost perfect. It just needed one final touch.

Master Sergeant Fields, I know uniform day is usually on Friday, but I need a small favor...

You're going to do great!

Just remember to breathe.

If you get nervous, look for us.

We'll be right in the front --

Guys! Stop before you make me more nervous!

Sorry! Get up there and kick butt!

I remembered why Dad and I always called Francine "the talker."

She didn't even need notes.

She sounded like she should be in a church pulpit...

Not a school assembly.

And I wasn't the only one who felt that way.

Maybe the words sounded right to them, too.

All day, people kept telling me I did a good job.

Even Master Sergeant Fields.

Things calmed down by the end of the day, and I almost forgot about the election.

Almost.

Maureen, Mr. Wilson would like to see you in his class.

He called you, too?

Yep. I guess that means one thing.

Come on in! Have a seat!

Where's everyone else?

Given the circumstances, I wanted to give you two the results before we announce them tomorrow morning.

Just in case things get emotional.

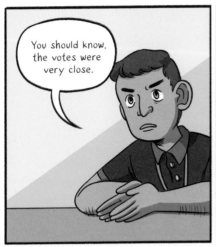

You should know, the votes were very close.

Closer than I've ever seen in a student council election.

But at the end of the day, there has to be a winner.

Maureen...

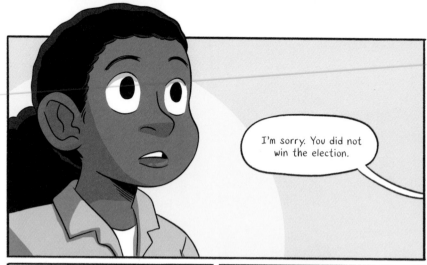

I'm sorry. You did not win the election.

It's okay if you want to cry.

It's totally understandable.

Maureen? Didn't you hear --

My sister lost?

But she worked so hard!

Why are you crying? You won!

Are you sure? Can you do a recount?

Maybe we can share the position.

No! You worked hard, too! You deserve it!

I'm so proud of you!

No, I'm proud of you!

This keeps getting stranger and stranger...

Better hurry up. Everyone will be here soon.

It won't take me long! Promise!

"Everyone" was Nikki, Tasha, Monique, and Amber. And Richard.

At least, that was our crew for tonight. We were pretty fluid.

You know Dad's going to take a billion pictures.

I bet you five dollars that he cries before we leave.

Ten.

I HEARD THAT!

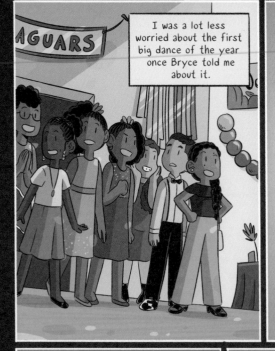

I was a lot less worried about the first big dance of the year once Bryce told me about it.

He's my seventh-grade buddy.

And yes, as others have said, he's very cute.

Hey, Maureen. Do you want to dance?

Maybe even boyfriend cute.

Maybe later? There's someone else I promised to dance with first.

ACKNOWLEDGMENTS

Many thanks to:

My agent, Sara Crowe, and my editors, Cassandra Pelham Fulton and Nick Thomas, for helping to turn this prose writer into a graphic novelist.

David Saylor, Carmen Alvarez, Lizette Serrano, Emily Heddleson, Danielle Yadao, Elisabeth Ferrari, along with so many others at Scholastic, for your continued support of my career.

Shannon Wright, for bringing Maureen, Francine, and the crew to life in ways that exceeded expectations in every way possible.

Jenni Holm, Gene Yang, Shannon Hale, and Raina Telgemeier, for your guidance on graphic novel scripts and process.

My Beverly Shores crew, for your early feedback on this project.

My family, as always, for your everlasting support.

And finally — Brad and Andrea, and Savannah and Sydney — for gifting me with a lifetime of stories. While this novel isn't a memoir, the emotions — and the love — are real and true.

VARIAN

With my twin, Brad, and sister, Andrea.
We're nine and she's five.

Many thanks to:

My agent, Hannah Mann, for always keeping me grounded, and my editors Cassandra Pelham Fulton and Nick Thomas. I made my first graphic novel!

David Saylor, Carmen Alvarez, Lizette Serrano, Emily Nguyen, Phil Falco, Shivana Sookdeo, and all the folks at Scholastic for being in my corner.

Varian Johnson for trusting me with his story — our girls Maureen and Francine and this vast world of characters — and for truly collaborating with me. Thank you.

My friends, both physically present and online, for constantly looking over my work, and for providing feedback, mental support, and love during such a tedious process. You all mean the world to me.

To my colorists: Andrea Bell, Damali Beatty, and Lauren Pierre.

My flatters: Amara Sherm, Ameorry Luo, Dhurata Mehmetja, Jasmine Walls, Kyle Katterjohn, Laura Arce, Leila Arisa, and Sierra Wilson.

My whole family, specifically my mom and dad, for the constant support that has never wavered. Not now, not when I was a little girl, not ever.

Kelly Alder, who I consider my comics mentor (and my second Dad). You were the catalyst, along with Chris Kindred, for my interest and career in comics. I've been grateful for every critique and form of guidance.

And finally, to Brandon Robertson. I wish you could have seen my first graphic novel, the same one you always told me I was working too hard on. The same one you provided so many gummies for during work sessions at my place. And the same one that has remnants of you scattered throughout. I did it, Brando!

SHANNON

With my little brother, Kevin (but we call him Duke), and cousin, Devin. I'm four and they're three.

VARIAN JOHNSON is the author of nine novels, including *The Parker Inheritance*, which was a Coretta Scott King Honor Book and a Boston Globe–Horn Book Award Honor Book, and *The Great Greene Heist*, which was an ALA Notable Children's Book and a Kirkus Reviews Best Book of 2014. He received an MFA from Vermont College of Fine Arts, where he now serves as a member of the faculty. Varian lives outside of Austin, Texas, with his family. To learn more, visit him online at varianjohnson.com.

SHANNON WRIGHT is an illustrator and cartoonist based in Richmond, Virginia. She has illustrated two picture books, *My Mommy Medicine* by Edwidge Danticat and *I'm Gonna Push Through* by Jasmyn Wright. She also provided the cover art for *Betty Before X* by Ilyasah Shabazz and Renée Watson, and *Strange Birds: A Field Guide to Ruffling Feathers* by Celia C. Pérez. Shannon graduated with a BFA from Virginia Commonwealth University, where she co-teaches a comics course during the summer. To learn more, visit her online at shannon-wright.com.